Notions in Rhyme
Poems

By
Fred J. Hoyle Sr.

fredjackhoyle@yahoo.com

ISBN 978-0-578-53847-1

Special Thanks to Ann Shuford

Contents

Sunset Angel 4

The Legend of the Broad River Ghost 6

Rutherford Jails Hanging Man's Shadow 8

The Ghost of Lisenberry Mountain.................................10

Axe Murder December 13, 1911 12

Angels of the Rainbow...14

A Ghostly Trick..16

Guardian Angel 20

The Eagle's Fish...22

Blue Dragon 24

"Knobby" South Mountains Big Foot..............................26

Too Smart...28

Ode to a Raindrop 30

Remember the Lawndale Dummy Line 34

The Reaper Came a Creeping 36

The Reaper's Touch 37

Pondering the Facets of My Ceasing to Be 38

A Grave Realization 39

Wounded 42

We Have Such Little Time Left Together......................45

Vacation 46

The Path Unseen 48

The Grim Creeper 49

The Fairy Ring 50

The Biggest Grin 52

Spring Flowers 53

Opossum in the Road 55

Oceans can Fly 56

Love Eternal 57

Let the Roses Bee 58

Hidden Grace 59

Grey Squirrel 60

Ghost of Glaciers..61

Earths Guest 62

Earth is a Free Will World 63

Dreamscape Space 64

Creations of Art...65

Awakening 66

About the Author..68

Sunset Angel
Fred J. Hoyle

Passing through the pearly gates
An angel enters heaven.
She beckons loudly to the Lord
Her boldness is forgiven.

With kind eyes he smiles at her
Saying all is well.
Many of your friends are here with me
Visit for a spell.

Thanks but I must go she says.
He wrinkles his brow.
Oh Heaven is beautiful
A real majestic wow.

But I must tell everyone
About this beautiful place.
Heaven lies above their heads.
Not just empty space.

When the Lord looks like he's moved
Her face starts beaming.
You can't go back to earth he says.
Her tears begin streaming.

The Lord's heart begins to ache.
He looks at her and sighs.
There's one thing that you can do
You can paint their skies.

It would be best at sunset
Clouds of red and silver
Patches streaks and shades of blue
Flowing like a river.

Don't forget black and orange
Give them all a try.
The angel smiles and spins around
Heading for the sky.

Smiling she swirls and mixes with glee
Colors glow and shine.
People on earth look up and see
Heaven is really divine.

All the angels stop and marvel.
The Lord gives a sigh.
She holds out the dripping brush
For others to give a try.

Beautiful art now fills the sky
Almost every day.
Keep an eye on the sunset
And watch the angels play.

It could be your loved one
That holds the brush.
Don't miss their masterpiece
Living in a rush.

The Legend of the Broad River Ghost
Fred J. Hoyle

Years ago, in old Broad River
A powerful fish did swim.
People came from miles around
To put a hook in him.
Broken rods and twisted lines
Increase the fish's fame.
Many men tugged for hours
But victory they couldn't claim.
The fish was given a demonic name,
Devil of the Night.
Lanterns twinkled along the river,
Until morning light.
A loving father brought his son
To teach him how to fish.
Being only ten years old
He wanted the devil fish.
They went to the river twice a week
And practiced every day.
He learned how to bait his hook
So nothing could get away.
Fishing one day on the river bank
The sun was shining bright.
The weather was perfect to catch some fish
Before the coming night.
The sun was setting in the west.
His boy got a bite.
I believe you've hooked the devil fish.
Hold on really tight.
The boy pulled with all his strength.
It jerked him into the flow.
His father screamed and grabbed for him
Yelling, "Let it go!"

Soon his son was out of sight.
Deeper and deeper he sank.
The next day the man was found
Weeping on the bank.
The man searched day and night
Until he finally dies.
According to the River legend
They couldn't close his eyes.
They buried him in a shallow grave
All of his friends cried.
When they returned he had dug out
From the inside.
They followed his trail toward the river
Where it disappeared.
They decided he was hiding beneath the water.
At least that's how it appeared.
Never go to the Broad alone
Late in the night.
The father may walk up on you
And he's a frightful sight.
With hair dangling from his skull
And eyes glaring too.
"Have you seen my little boy?"
He'll scream at you!
You better think twice before you go
It may not be much fun.
He wants to return to his grave
With his beloved son.
If you look like his little boy
There's little you can do.
His finger bones are very sharp
And he'll hook you.

Rutherford Jails Hanging Man's Shadow
Fred J. Hoyle

In the year of eighteen-eighty
Mr. Daniel Kieth.
Enjoyed his life in Rutherford County
As a petty thief.
He swindled men out of their money
Selling his gold mine.
In Rutherford county at that time
It was an easy crime.
He pulled them in when he showed them stones
From his secret place.
He forgot to mention that it was brass
Scratched upon their face.
The money was gone when the men learned
That the deal was shady.
They got their chance to punish him
In January of eighteen-eighty.
The body of Alice Ellis was found
Lying in a wooded field.
A witness saw him drunk and rowdy
Near where she was killed.
Quickly the sheriff went to his house
Hoping to learn more.
Blood was splattered on Daniel's shirt
When he opened his door
Daniel swore it was that of a rabbit
He was going to skin.
Because he had such a bad reputation
The sheriff took him in.
He claimed his innocence every day.
Everyone turned their head.
He had no chance in the Rutherford court.
"He's guilty," the jury said.
He appealed to a higher N.C. court.
Their decision seemed shady.

The Judge said that he would be hanged
In December of eighteen-eighty.
Daniel was returned to Rutherford jail
To spend a sad day.
He had to sit and look at his coffin
Until they took him away.
He told the sheriff that fateful day
That he was truly innocent.
His soul won't ever rest in peace
Until he proves he's innocent.
He growled at the sheriff before he was hung
His voice wasn't faint.
"A man should be hung for what he's done
Not for what he ain't."
As Daniel stepped up to the gallows
He turned to the sheriff and said.
"Keep your cool and don't get excited."
Then he held up his head.
Not long after he was hung
His spirit came to call.
The shadow of a hanging man
Appeared on the jail's wall.
The sheriff thought it was a prank
And painted over it.
It went away but Daniel Kieth
Made another hit.
There was nothing they could do
To make it go away.
The mark of shame was on that wall
Until demolition day.
Daniel didn't haunt the jail
Just because of spite.
He only wanted to prove to the world
That he was right.

The Ghost of Lisenberry Mountain

Fred J. Hoyle

Golden Valley is a beautiful place
Still wild and untamed.
If you're willing to work real hard
There's gold there to be claimed.
Hardy men once dug all day
And panned in her streams.
They put their gold in leather pouches
Fulfilling their dreams.
The assay office bought the gold.
Into the safe it went.
When the safe could hold no more
They sent it to Bechtler's mint.
It wasn't long before evil men
No different from any pirate.
Knew which stagecoach had the gold
And made plans to acquire it.
When the time was right they attacked.
The coach was well on its way.
All the riders and most of the guards
Went to heaven that day.
Several guards riding on horses
Managed to get away.
Staying hidden they followed the thieves
For the rest of the day.
They watched the thieves climb up the side
Of Lisenberry Mountain.
The thieves went straight to a hidden cave
And slithered into the mountain.
Two guards hid to watch the entrance
Of their getaway.
Another hurried to get some help
For the next day.
The thieves drank and sang all night.
Hidden within the mountain.
Music and laughter flowed from the entrance

Like an endless fountain.
The next day the guard returned
With a marshal and men.
They yelled for the thieves to come out.
A shot rang from within!
Two days later the marshal went in
With many torches lit.
They didn't travel very far
Before the torches quit.
Unable to breathe they barely got out
As music came from inside.
The lawmen tried again and again
Until two of them died.
The marshal decided the gold was lost
And the thieves were probably dead.
He told his men to seal the entrance.
"This place is cursed," he said.
Many men have searched the mountain
Digging and scratching around.
They all want to find the gold
Hidden under its ground.
Now when men hear the legend
They search the mountain's face.
But the entrance that hides the gold
Is gone without a trace.
If you're curious and visit the mountain
Go halfway to the top.
As the sun goes down you'll hear
The music that no one can stop.
Don't take a shovel if you go
Especially late at night.
The ghost will open up the entrance
And snatch you out of sight!
They'll drag you deep into the mountain
Where you can see the gold.
But none of this will matter to you
Because you'll be stiff and cold.

Axe Murder December 13, 1911

Fred J. Hoyle

In the year of nineteen-eleven
On December thirteen.
The devil took a little trip
To do something mean.

He came upon a town named Fallston
In Cleveland County.
Everyone there worked hard
Harvesting nature's bounty.

He couldn't just leave them alone
And pass on by.
A nice young prosperous farmer
Caught his evil eye.

The farmer seemed to have some money
And that would make it easy.
With plenty of other men around
He found some that were sleazy.

He took control of all their minds
So they would do his will.
No one knows exactly which one
He chose to make the kill.

They used the blunt end of an axe
The devil was thrilled.
The devil wanted more excitement
And had his wife killed.

The farmer's daughter was so young
She was left unharmed.
Then the devil went to work
He made the neighbors alarmed.

They accused lots of men
And one of them did confess.
He implicated several more
It was a real mess.

Even though the devil moved on
He left his evil spell.
By the time the courts were through
One man was in jail.

No one knew if he really did it
His stories were so crazy.
When the farmer's daughter grew old
The facts were still hazy.

Then in July of nineteen-eighty
She got to know the truth.
She went to heaven where her mom and dad
Hugged their baby Ruth.

Angels of the Rainbow

Fred J. Hoyle

God once sent a massive flood
To wash earth's evil away.
Only those on Noah's ark
Were alive at the end of the day.
Other creatures and evil men
Release their souls to rise.
All of them ascend to heaven
To stand before God's eyes.
The men bow their weary heads
Full of earnest shame.
They have no choice but to except
The devil's cruel flame.
The children tremble except for one
And he looks up to God.
Speaking strong but humbly
He pleads to God.
Please spare our little souls
We never grew up.
Let us prove ourselves to you
Take away this cup.
God looks down and shakes his head
Then gives his reply.
I know you never got the chance
Before you had to die
Maybe I should send you back
But I can't right now.
The earth is still covered with water
He sighs with a wrinkled brow.
This is a problem says the Lord
I won't do this again.
The child smiles and says to God
Thank you Lord amen.

God looks toward earth's sky
And makes a promise to man.
Then decides to give him a sign
High above the land.
I'll make angels of this group
If you all agree.
Here is what I expect of you
Listen carefully.
Now and then when it rains on earth
You'll light up a rainbow.
Your halos will be of many colors
When I call you'll go.
Beautiful and faint until you all arrive
Then it will brightly glow.
Magnificent and large to assure all men
On the earth below.
I'll never allow a massive flood
To wash all life away.
Men won't need an ark again
After this day.
The children bow in humble respect.
God's heart sings.
He lights their halos of different colors
And gives them all their wings.
The children make such sweet angels
That God is moved.
Never again will a child have to worry
Their place in heaven is approved.
The Rainbow Angels serve our lord
In a special way.
A beautiful place is waiting for them
On judgment day.

A Ghostly Trick
Fred J. Hoyle

I once discovered an old house
Rotting to the ground.
Intrigued and curious I stayed a while
To look around.

Its curtains tattered and windows cracked.
The door was gone in the back.
I felt a presence calling me
To enter the old shack.

Even though it was dark inside
I felt there was no threat.
I spent some time milling around
And found a place to set.

I don't think I imagined it
But things were shown to me.
Stories of those who lived in the house
I could plainly see.

I shed a tear as I went outside
And slowly strolled away.
Then a spirit touched my hand.
 I didn't know what to say.

I tried to persuade it to go back
Before we went too far.
But the presence was still strong
When I reached my car.

Upon returning to my house
I wanted to share my day.
My wife just shook her head at me
And turned away.

The eerie feeling faded away
Until that night.
I felt the presence in my house
It gave me a fright.

Tired and not in the mood to worry
I went to bed.
Sleeping soundly, I saw the shack
Plainly in my head.

Then a voice spoke to me.
I rubbed my weary eyes.
The spirit was lying by my side.
I gasp in surprise.

Calm yourself and do not worry
Every thing's alright.
I can only talk for a minute
Until tomorrow night.

The next day I wondered if
It had been a dream.
But when the spirit woke me again
I was about to scream.

Then the spirit spoke softly to me.
"Please excuse the fright.
I can only speak for a minute
And only at midnight.

Once I loved a wonderful man
It was long ago.
He died first and went to heaven
I waited too long to go.

Now I'm stuck here on the earth
Inside that shack.
You can easily set me free
Just burn the shack.

I know he's sad as he waits for me
I didn't understand.
He can never return to the shack
Things got out of hand.

Burn the shack so I can go to heaven
I see your concern.
Let me go to the man I love
Make the shack burn."

She never came back again
It made me feel sad.
Finally I decided to burn the shack
Even if that's bad.

I hid in the woods while it burned
So no one would see.
Then someone kissed my cheek
I figured she was free.

That night as I lay in bed
Her voice was loud and clear
"Thanks for helping me and my friends
Now we all live here.

No one's in heaven waiting for me.
I hated to trick you.
But our house was almost gone
I did what I had to do."

Guardian Angel
Fred J. Hoyle

Quite a few years ago
Far from earth.
A lovely angel asked our Lord
To let her prove her worth.
The Lord smiled at her and replied
Stay here instead.
I would hate to see you leave.
Then she shook her head.
I yearn to be a guardian angel
Share the things I know.
It would be such an honor
To watch a child grow.
If you'll let me do this task
I'll gladly guide him through.
He'll be safe and have a chance
To get to know you.
The Lord grants the angel her wish
And off to Earth she goes.
Why she landed beside my mother
Only the Lord knows.
I also came to earth that night
Filled with fear and scorn.
My mother and the angel smiled at me
The moment that I was born.
My Mother snuggled and comforted me
And I felt her love.
The angel stayed by our side
A gift from above.
When I grew a little older
I could feel her near.
She did her best to keep me safe
Her purpose was always clear.
Then at a point later in life
I knew everything.

I hardly thought about her at all
Until one lovely spring.
A wonderful girl came into my life
We truly fell in love.
Soon we started a family.
I thanked the Lord above.
Then I asked for an angel like mine
To watch our child so dear.
I think I heard my angel say
They're already here.
As time passed quickly by
My angel stayed near.
Many times I thanked her for
A relationship so dear.
Then one evening I went to bed
On a peaceful night.
Suddenly I saw my angel's face
What a beautiful sight.
She was there with my mother
Standing by my side.
My mother and the angel smiled at me
The night that I died.
Quite a few years passed by
Far from earth.
Now an angel I ask the lord
To let me prove my worth.
I want to be a guardian angel
Share the things I know.
It would be such an honor
To watch a child grow.

The Eagle's Fish
Fred J. Hoyle

An eagle spies a great big fish
Washed upon a shore.
Quickly diving he grapples the prize
A feast is in store.

Nearby a crow is watching
And cocks his head.
The fish looks so wonderful
"I'll steal a bite," he said.

Feeling something tug from behind
The eagle turns and glares.
The crow jumps back wobbling his head
Squawking as he stares.

Strong and mad the eagle attacks
The crow flies away.
As the eagle tears at the fish
The crow decides to play.

Spying another crow nearby
He flies up to his limb.
See that eagle with a fish
Let's eat it for him.

The other crow smirks and sighs
That could be a pain.
We're not going to fight with him
We're going to use our brain

You take east and I'll take west
I'll catch his sight.
When he takes off after me
You can steal a bite.

When he stops chasing me
He's going to see you.
While he's running you away
I'll steal a few.

The other crow nods with a smile
It just might work.
Let's go make a big fool
Of that jerk.

The first crow flutters as he lands
In the eagle's face.
The other crow quietly lands
Taking his place.

The game begins in deadly earnest
And last for a while.
When they finally end the skirmish
Both crows smile

Proud he ran the crows away
The eagle struts around.
Until he looks toward his prize
Lying on the ground.

Too arrogant throughout the fight
He didn't realize.
The crows had eaten all his fish
Before they hit the skies.

Blue Dragon

Fred J. Hoyle

Shiny blue dragons once flew in the skies
A beautiful thing to see
Sailing above the wilderness
Their lives were carefree

A sea of green covered the ground
An endless canopy
So thick was the forest below
No danger could they see

But cunning and cold cave-men lived
Hiding out of sight
They had to hunt for food and fur
Both day and night.

The dragons were content to flourish
Living off the land
They had no desire to cut a tree
They liked what nature had planned

Men were restless to change things
And simple tools were made
Chipping at stones by their firelight
They fashioned a flint blade

Meadows appeared in the canopy
As trees disappeared
When dragons landed in the grassy meadows
Dangerous men appeared

The dragons were caught by surprise
When their arrows flew
Dying dragons fell to the ground
And many men died too

Dragons tried to keep to themselves
By hiding from mankind.
Men chose to hunt them down
And kill all they find

Dragons had to defend their den
Killing many men
Angry men built bigger bows
And they begin to win

Men lusting for a quest
Tracked the dragons down
Dragons found no place to hide
Men were all around

Many dragons were put in cages
With broken hearts they died
Shiny blue dragons no longer fly
And none are left to hide

"Knobby" South Mountains Big Foot

Fred J. Hoyle

Near Casar in the South Mountains
Carpenters knob does set.
There a big foot roams around
Causing the locals to fret
But they all put up with him
And call him Knobby.
He stays hidden most of the time
Because his hair is so globby.
Now that Knobby is famous
They think he's really fine.
A dozen people saw him
In nineteen seventy-nine.
He's slightly taller than most men
And covered with hair.
People say there is at least
Four inches there.
Unlike big foot of the west
His hair is kind a light.
But like his allusive cousins
His feet are quite a sight.
He has never hurt anyone.
That's not his way.
Once he visited a local man
For a whole day.
I found this man so we could talk
He'd had a drink.
He says that Knobby is getting old
Then sits to think.
"I'll tell you what Knobby had to say.
 He shared a lot with me.
His world is nothing like ours
Now listen carefully.
There are only a few Knobbys

For you to behold.
They only replace themselves
When they're too old.
Claiming to be three hundred years old
He offered me his job.
I chuckled rolled my eyes and said
Now come on Knob.
Then Knobby tried to explain
That there is a weed.
That all Knobbys know about
From ageing I'll be freed.
I asked him why he's getting too old
If he's so clever.
Knobby looked at me and smirked
You can't live forever.
If you decide to take this job
Your body will renew.
But your hair and feet will grow
And people will stare at you.'
I got my jug and smiled at him
Then I took a sip.
Knobby decided to try my drink
He did a double flip.
We laughed and talked for a while
I gave him a jug to keep.
Then I took a really big drink
And lay down to sleep.
My head was spinning when I woke
And Knobby was gone.
I went to get another jug
But they were all gone.
The next morning, I went to work
Moonshine I need.
Next time I fetched a jug
On top of them lay a weed."

Too Smart
Fred J. Hoyle

Population is on the rise
More men appear
Reproducing reproducing
More men appear

Houses spring up everywhere
Forests disappear
Tilling more and more land
Forests disappear

Domestic animals are everywhere
Wild ones die
Hybrid crops grow and grow
Wild ones die

The world is losing its honey bees
They're almost gone
Fossil fuels are burning fast
They're almost gone

God who created man so smart
Doesn't understand
Why a creature created to think
Doesn't understand

Mother Nature is on her knees
But she's going to stand
Man so smart will hold her down
But she's going to stand

She will knock us to the ground
We will wonder why
God will only shake his head
We will wonder why

When we've destroyed this beautiful earth
God will cry
Starving men will slowly die
God will cry

The sin of killing earth forgiven
Only with God's grace
The population of heaven will rise
Only with God's grace

Ode to a Raindrop
Fred J. Hoyle

Floating peacefully above our heads
So beautiful pure and clean
A crystal-clear drop of water
Can hardly be seen

Content to finally escape the sea
It longs to rest a while
But nature has a different plan
She looks at it with a smile

"O little drop of water you know
Others are counting on you
It's time to begin your journey again."
Then away it flew

Sucked up by a determined wind
It was tossed and swirled
Rising high into the sky
Into a crystal it curled

Fluttering wildly and bright white
The little flake of snow
Shivers as it makes its way
Back to the earth below

Angry clouds throw spears of light
Toward the thirsty ground
The flake of snow begins to melt
Turning juicy and round

Hitting the sod with a mighty splat
It slithers out of sight
Soaking down into the earth
The end of its life in flight

A withered plant opens its eyes
As the drop slides by
The drop smiles as the plant turns green
And then says goodbye

Content to have helped the plant
It longs to rest a while
But nature has a different plan
She looks at it with a smile

"Many others are counting on you
Surely you must know
It's time to begin your journey again
Reach out and join a flow."

Coursing through the veins of earth
Moving out of sight
Growing beautiful pure and clean
And then there is light

Blinded by the bright sunshine
Many drops rise
With their journey cut short
They return to the skies

The helpless little drop of water
Is hidden within the flow
It cringes as it's tossed about
Caught in a treacherous flow

Finally, the drop of water sighs
The flow has really grown
Mighty wide and deep now
It picks a path of its own

The drop of water almost laughs
When tickled by a fish
Feeling content the fish moves on
Spinning the drop with a swish

Floating with many droplet friends
Lots of creatures swim by
Nature smiles and looks at him
"Without you they would die."

Time passes and the river slows
The drop can hardly be seen
The river is heavy with dirt and silt
And the drop's no longer clean

Nature looks at the little drop
"Your river life is through.
The mighty ocean lies ahead
Soon it will swallow you."

In the distance a familiar sound
Continues to grow louder
Mighty waves crash like thunder
Beating everything into powder

The drop of water is striped clean
And turned into brine
It drifts far out to sea
Watching the sun shine

The drop of water feels strange
And begins to wonder why
When it finally figures it out
It's high up in the sky

Floating peacefully above our heads
So beautiful pure and clean
The crystal-clear drop of water
Can hardly be seen

Remember the Lawndale Dummy Line
Fred J. Hoyle

Drift with me into the past
We'll board a little train.
A train that almost everyone loved
Though it was very plain.

It was old when it came to town
In eighteen ninety-nine.
Bought by Major H. S. Schenck
To him it looked fine.

The train would bring coal and cotton
To Cleveland Textile mill.
With hardly any roads to Shelby
It wouldn't set still.

He started off with two little engines
And ten freight cars.
But people begged to ride to Shelby
Because they had no cars.

Good news came in nineteen and three.
People could finally ride.
But with only two passenger cars
Most people rode outside.

The open coaches were a hit
When the weather was good.
But sometimes it was rainy and cold
They did the best they could.

The people of Lawndale fell in love
And called it the Dummy Line.
The miles of track weren't very long
They only totaled nine.

The engine was pretty and kinda small
Almost like a toy.
It puffed and chugged down a beautiful track
Riding it was a joy.

The train ran forward as it chugged to Shelby
But backed as it returned.
Delivering goods up and down the line
It paid for the coal it burned.

The Dummy Line was a success
For forty-four years.
And when it reached the end of the line
Many people shed tears.

They miss the song of the Dummy Line
Clack, clack roll---clack clack roll.
The rhythm of travel they loved is gone
Clack, clack roll---clack clack roll.

Close your eyes and remember when.
Clack, clack roll---clack clack roll
Clack, clack roll---clack clack roll
Clack, clack roll.

The Reaper Came a Creeping
Fred J. Hoyle

Death crept down my hall one night
Like a shadow even in no light
It slid beneath my bedroom door
And eased across the wooden floor
It looked at me with stone-cold eyes
Propped up its sickle and began to rise
Aware that a presence was near
I opened my eyes in great fear
He squinted those eyes, taking it in
I started to fight, but I could never win
Peace to you, was all I could say
His expression changed in a curious way
He pushed back his hood and cocked his head
Are you not troubled that soon you will be dead?
It's just the price we pay for life, I said.
He smiled a bit and rubbed his chin
I'm leaving now but I will be back again
I thanked him for letting me see another day
He shook his head and began fading away
Whispering I heard him say
One day you will beg me to come this way
You will be feeble and your friends will be too
But that's the price you pay for the gift I just gave you.

The Reaper's Touch
Fred J. Hoyle

Lying in my weary death bed
Pain throbbing from my toes to my head
Some people come to my side to talk
Others just come by to gawk
Even though life was lots of fun
It's time for my spirit to break loose and run
Just when I can stand no more
A skull in a cloak enters my door
He eases close to my bedside
His fearful scythe he does not hide
With pain raging I look into his eyes
He touches my hand and what a surprise
Everything in the room disappears
I feel wonderful and wipe my tears
My pain vanishes without a trace
His eyes soften and the skull becomes a face
He smiles at me and begins to glow
Whispering he says it's time to go
I flinch as we pass through the bedroom ceiling
Oh, but that was a wonderful feeling
We sail out into the moonlit night
I notice his scythe is in plain sight
Why do you still have that weapon, I said?
He smiles at me as he turns his head
Even the angel of death could be attacked
If we are the devil will get whacked
It's my job to get you safely through the light
Then I will disappear into the night

Pondering the Facets of My Ceasing to Be
Fred J. Hoyle

Here I sit pondering the facets of my ceasing to be
Will death look me in the face and tease me to worry
Or could it be so kind as to quench my flame quick as
a smack
I hope that day does not dash upon me as if in a hurry
But ceasing to be, at this point in life, is garnished with
little fear
Life has been a feast for body and soul, it has been
grand
Turmoil, trials, and some distress always eased with
prayer
And love, sweet love has always been close at hand
I found the jewel that God cut for me and she gave me
three more
We danced and loved, discovered and cried side by
side on this stage
O, but death, I know too well where I will feel your
sting
Should the angel of death take only me from this page
It will not matter that heaven is vast, amazing, and
grand
The place will be lonely as hell until I once again hold
my jewel's hand

A Grave Realization
Fred J. Hoyle

Compelled to walk one lovely day I left with no path in mind.
I passed a beautiful, oh so peaceful graveyard.
Filled with mystique, it caused me to stop and ponder.
It was an old one, with lovely monuments placed so carefully.
Like little pyramids to remind us that those laid beneath their shadows were once as important as any pharaoh.
But now, those who rest there are dust, and so are their descendants.
Nature is reclaiming the yard.

I traveled on with mind in thought.
A beautiful green meadow loomed ahead.
Large plaques of bronze lying in its grass dotted the scene.
Many were adorned with cups filled with plastic flowers
Compelled to enter this graveyard, I strolled about.
It wasn't as old, but peaceful, and the imitation flowers were quite colorful.
Its mystique was not as strong, but I could feel its presence.
All the graves looked the same, unless I paused to read a plaque.
Those who rest below that sod are almost dust, but nature is still held at bay.
It's easy to mow over plaques

As I left, I was drawn to a new graveyard
standing neatly on a hill.
Columns and walls surrounded a courtyard with no grass at all,

The structure is a solitary monument, made up of
pockets covered with little brass plates.
They all are perfectly aligned.
I only felt its mystique when I closed my eyes in
meditation.
Not all pockets held urns, but speckled about were
plates with names inscribed on them.
Behind those plates, held in place by tiny brass screws,
lies the dust of people who were as dearly loved as
those resting under little pyramids in graveyards of old.

Troubled by its simplicity, I chose a courtyard bench
and sit to lament.
Were those buried long ago more precious than those
who pass now?
Oh, what does it matter to these poor souls?

A chill prickles my spine.
Has man come to realize that monuments, plaques, and
columns will in time be dust, too?
Even this rock sphere that birthed and fed millions
upon millions of bodies with souls will one day be as
dead as all those she nourished.
It will become a beautiful monument shining in space
for a while, but earth will not escape without all her
mass being bashed into dust again.
That dust will be scattered to the far ends of the
universe where it will return to the storeroom of God,
and he will build other worlds with all our dust.

Gripped in hopelessness, I searched my soul.
I closed my eyes and allowed the mystique of the
graveyards to guide my thoughts.
In peaceful contemplation I realized that our souls are
not made of dust.
They are as eternal as God's breath from which they
are made, and everything will be fine.

Wounded

Fred J. Hoyle

On a beautiful day in 1865
Eighteen years old I was so alive
The sound of battle thrilled part of me
Death lay all around but I did not see
My youthful confidence made me brave
Every ounce of energy I freely gave
Taking chances filled my veins with zeal
I lost all compassion as I made kill after kill
A bullet a thud I shrieked in pain
Too late I realized this was all insane
My head was spinning as I stumbled away
I plopped to the ground where other men lay
A wagon stopped and we crawled on board
We found some medics but we were ignored
We wrapped our wounds as best we could
The wagon bounced away and there we stood
Our side was defeated by the end of the day
Our only hope was to run away
I trudged toward home on a cruel trail
With six more men all wounded and frail
We crossed a stream and drank water again
But food can't be caught by helpless men
Most were to sick to eat anyway
And several were hot on this cold, cold day
That night in the woods the feverish men cried
And when the sun rose, they all had died
All of us that could did our very best
To lay our friends respectfully to rest

We all shed tears as we walked away
And I walked pretty well for half of the day
But I knew something was wrong when I began to sweat
My head ached and my clothes were dripping wet
When we stopped for the night, I laid down and cried
I was too weak to help as another man died
Two men struggled to get him into the ground
My body trembled and my heart began to pound
When morning came I awoke with a smile
I watched the sun as it rose for a while
The men stood up and looked at me
One came over and kneeled on a knee
I said good morning to him and stood
He stayed on his knee and then I understood
I saw myself curled up on the ground
I tried to speak there but was no sound
They picked me up and there was no pain
I watch as they bury me and there was no pain
Even as under the sod I lay
I could see them as they walked away
Tears fell from my dirty eyes
The moment I began to realize
How much pain they both will see
Until they finally rest like me
I'm comfortable here in my earthly bed
Is this a dream or am I really dead
The first night the stars were amazingly bright
I lay and marveled at them all night
When the sun rose I wasn't sleepy at all
So I spent the day watching the trees so tall
I know I'm lucky to be laying out here
Nature's beautiful and I have nothing to fear
Night brought a wolf close to my bed
He sniffed and sniffed above my head

The next day there was no sun to shine
It drizzled and rained but I felt fine
I heard every drop as they hit the ground
They made a melodic pleasing sound
I hope my friend that's buried nearby
Is peaceful and as happy out here as I
Contently I watch as time passes by
Except for the day I heard my mother cry
One of the men that buried me
Brought her here because she wanted to see
The place where her son was laid in the ground
She came pretty close but they never found
Exactly where my flowers should lay
I watched intently as they walked away
Much time had passed since I shed a tear
But that night I cried as I lay out here
The morning sun took my sadness away
And now I'm just waiting for judgment day

We Have Such Little Time Left Together
Fred J. Hoyle

With sad eyes my wife looked at me and said
We have such little time left together
Hundreds of thoughts ran through my head
We reached out and hugged each other

With kind eyes I looked at her and said
When in heaven we'll find each other
And then there's one thing that will never be
said
We have such little time left together

Vacation
Fred J. Hoyle

Time, passing in peace
Rest so much rest
I'm tired of resting
I'm tired of endless days
I do love my friends
Friendships so eternal
Music here is divine
I need a change, excitement
I prayed for a lark
Where would you go? I hear.
Earth looks beautiful, I reply
Earth is intriguing, I say.
The world of dirt? I hear.
Yes I replied.
I drifted almost unconscious
Slowly my sight begins to work
Tender love I soak in
No control of where I go
Love and play
I don't understand anyone
Time helps me learn
Playing with fellow members of humanity
Pain and tears
I learn to fit in
Time passing faster now
Learning about a thing called life
Things to explore
Emotions galore
More to learn the hard way

Then, oh then, Love
I bring more to visit this place
A different, but sweet love for them
This world is really made of dirt
A wonderful playground made of dirt
Much time passes
Not as much fun, but I still love being loved
Then one I love leaves
Then another, another
Lonely much of the time
Pain and tears but nothing to learn
Losing control
Growing faint
Beautiful memories from the planet of dirt
Many tears and good byes
I drifted almost unconscious
Bright light and beautiful music
Peace and rest
Did you enjoy life? I hear.
Life?
Yes, life is your vacation
From eternal existence.

The Path Unseen
Fred J. Hoyle

Behind our eyes a pathway lies
That's not beneath the earth's skies
A lovely path we often should take
For inner joy and sanity's sake.

It is a place where it's easy to pray
And look at ourselves in a different way
Relax and savor its heavenly bliss
Our soul's energy is increased by this

With closed eyes look the other way
Travel this path and let your soul play
Spiritual awareness and joy will swell
And you will know this path well

When our eyes can open no more
This path will be an open door
Fly to its end, grace and peace await
For this is the path to heaven's gate.

The Grim Creeper
Fred J. Hoyle

I would rather go with the grim reaper
Than to tangle with his brother the grim creeper
The reaper takes you away on sight
But his brother takes you bite by bite
He slowly nibbles away your brain
Giving your loved one's years of pain

The Fairy Ring
. Fred J. Hoyle

Awoke by a sound in the middle of the night
I slid out of bed and turned on a light
Its contagious rhythm beckoned me
To go outside and see what it could be
The moon was bright I would need no light
Empty handed I trudged into the night
Soon I could hear sweet harmony
In perfect pitch with this melody
The rhythm took control of my feet
And I marched along to the beat
Heading to a place hidden from sight
I began to see a glow of light
I parted branches and to my surprise
A ritual appeared before my eyes
Toads and frogs of every kind
All of them stoned out of their mind
Swaying together in harmony
A joyous amphibious community
Encircled by a ring of toad stools
Chirping and singing like a bunch of fools
Their harmony made such a beautiful sound
That I stayed to watch them dance around.
Then one of them caught a glimpse of me.
It screamed and ended their jubilee.
It pointed at me and they jerked around
Their eyes turned red big and round.
In unison they growled an evil sound.
My mouth dropped open and I took off with a
bound.

I dashed away like a streak of light
And disappeared into the night.
The next morning as I crawled out of bed.
What I had seen still danced in my head.
I decided to forget it and go to work
But stepping outside I turned with a jerk
In my yard stood an amazing thing.
A large and mysterious fairy ring.

The Biggest Grin
Fred J. Hoyle

The biggest grin you will ever see
Will be on an opossum
In a persimmon tree

A happier creature you will never see
With his mouth full of fruit
As he clings to the tree

Sleeping all day and playing at night
He stays out of the sun
And out of sight

Keep your distance and be polite
If you're ever near one
His fifty teeth bite

Spring Flowers

Fred J. Hoyle

Two spring flowers were you and I
When I picked you and you picked me
We shared our love in a beautiful meadow
That filled our lives with ecstasy

But deep inside, we needed more
Our love was real in this empty meadow
So we strived to make it the kind of place
Where little flowers could easily grow

We hoped and dreamed of things to come
Made vows of love we intended to keep
So together we pushed weeds out of our way
Content and happy our roots grew deep

Our summer was hot and how we bloomed
We hoped and dreamed that our seeds would
grow
Time passed quickly and showers came
Little flowers sprang up to and fro

We smiled dreamed and danced in the wind
As fall's cool breath came blowing in
Time had come that we would bloom no more
But our little flowers were blooming by then

We shivered smiled and shared our dreams
As winter swept over our beautiful meadow
Our little flowers lost all of their blooms
But their seeds are fertile and ready to grow

With dreams fulfilled the killing frost came
around
We surrendered in peace on that fateful day
Entwined in embrace we sank to the ground
And the wind with a swish just blew us away

Opossum in the Road
Fred J. Hoyle

An adventurous opossum finds an amazing trail
Like none he's ever seen
The woods on the other side look so swell
Everything is luscious and green

Half way across a beast comes along
He remembers what his mother said
Lay down, play dead, nothing will go wrong
Frightened he lays down his head

A big car swerves leaving him unharmed
With a Grin he's back on his way
As another beast approaches, he's less alarmed
He drops in the busy highway

The second car dodges him as most cars will
This ancient legend seems true
But a third car came and made the kill
These beasts don't care what your mother told
you

Oceans can Fly
Fred J. Hoyle

Thank God oceans can fly
Their restless waters fill the sky
Drifting far from their sea beds
Life giving water above our heads
Countless droplets bathe thirsty ground
Filling rivers and streams all around
Obedient to gravity back to sea they head
To watch waves dance above their bed.

J.

Love Eternal
Fred J. Hoyle

I have heard that nothing last forever
But I feel as if I know
That the love of God
And the love between two souls
Is eternal

Let the Roses Bee
Fred J. Hoyle

Fragrant little rose bush, how lovely you
sweeten the wind
With crimson buds unfolded in luscious bloom
A prickly young rose bush, savors the gesture
you send
His blooms are filled with pollen, and love does
loom
You yearn to caress or share a touch, but he
grows far up the hill
The honey bees once delivered his passion, but
their wings no longer hum.
Your lover's blossoms will hardly be touched,
and his pollen stays up the hill
Sadly you bloom and wait and wait, for love that
will never come

Hidden Grace
Fred J. Hoyle

The grace of God is hard to find
When without regard for those left behind
The Creator of energy mass and men
Calls home our loved ones again and again

Those who were in agony for quite some time
May smile as Jacob's ladder they climb
And those who leave at the speed of light
Feel little remorse with heaven in sight

Anger and scorn tempt those left behind
Blaming their creator for being unkind
But God cares deeply for every grieving soul
Disguised as time, his grace makes them
whole

Grey Squirrel
Fred J. Hoyle

Squirrels are born high in the trees
Their houses are made of sticks and leaves
A furry creature that's mostly tale
Feasting on nuts they live well

Never do we see one fall
As they chase each other in tree tops tall
Entertaining those who live on the ground
Little acrobats flipping and jumping around

Sometimes they stop to sit and fuss
Flip their tales and chatter at us
But when confronted while on the ground
They spring up a tree with a leap and a bound

They help themselves to the fruit on our trees
And empty birdfeeders with the greatest of ease
They're truly amazing in front of a car
Twisting and turning who knows where they are

But old grey squirrel means us no harm
And most of the time he's quite a charm
Hardly noticing that we are around
Though we're in the middle of his playground

Ghost of Glaciers
Fred J. Hoyle

Glaciers once slept upon earth's mountains
Peaceful and cold they crept to the sea
Awakened by sweat they trickle like fountains
Hastening their journey to the sea

The sea consumes them as they die
Gorging their water it burst at its sides
But the ghost of these glaciers will not lie
They rise in sea clouds providing them rides

Restless and free they are filling our skies
Their fathoms of tears whip the earth below
Energy that slept is awake in our skies
And until they sleep their wrath will grow.

Earths Guest
Fred J. Hoyle

Life is a journey for many souls
Others perceive it as a test
Problems and hurdles confront us all
That's part of being Earth's guest

\

Earth is a Free Will World
Fred J. Hoyle

Earth, the world of five senses
Why did we wake up here?
Some days are like a beautiful journey
Others are laden with fear

If this is a journey for adventurous souls
Did we ask to be Earths guest
Or is it our duty to struggle here
If we pass we're eternally blessed

We yearn to know the meaning of life
But we never really have control
Sure we can choose many paths
But bad luck takes its toll

Dreamscape Space
Fred J. Hoyle

Dreams of the dead are ghost
A transcendental trip at most
They visit because they miss you so
Most of the time you won't even know
But if you dream of them one night
And if by chance the timing is right
You will meet your loved one face to face
In the magical world of dreamscape space
Proof they are patiently waiting for you
To be together when your life is through

Creations of Art
Fred J. Hoyle

This universe is simply God's art gallery
Breathtaking colors shining and sparkling in
cold dark space
Immersed in a vastness that may have no end
With spiraling galaxies mixed in like flowers
strewn across a field
Stars shine and glow, putting on a show for their
destined time
All with different colors that God alone chooses
They turn and churn in a spectacle of fury and
fireworks
Even their deaths are artfully done as red giants
or super nova bangs
Oh but the wandering planets of unimaginable
numbers that spin and whirl
Most exist for no reason we could understand
Sculpted in every shape, size, and color, many
adorned with spots and storms
Holding in their clutches bright moons and rings
These planets are little art galleries suspended in
God's universe
Some filled with the beauty of life, probably no
two the same
Intelligent beings on these planets gaze at the
heavens in wonder and awe
Unknowingly praising his name

Awakening
Fred J. Hoyle

I'm lying in a tiny room
The last thing I heard was boom
Why I'm here I cannot tell
I have no taste I have no smell
How small can this room be
I cannot move I cannot see
I sense that others surround me
Where oh where can I be.

About the Author

Fred J. Hoyle was born in 1947 in Lawndale NC a little town nestled in the foothills of the South Mountains. With few neighbors close by, he explored the woods and creeks surrounding his family's farm. Energetic imagination provided adventure as he played in his own little wilderness. A love and respect for the beauty and reality of nature evolved. At age eleven his family moved to Shelby where he attended Shelby High School and Gardner Webb College. While in college he discovered that Business administration was a gateway to a different kind of adventure. Fred fell in love with a wonderful woman and they raised three amazing children.

Now with more free time, he has discovered that with pen in hand he can once again use his imagination to venture into natures beautiful woods. Endless dangers and triumphs wait to be savored. He is the author of *Dragons of Venosta*, and *The Great Dragoll War*. They are both available at Amazon books.